ZONDERKIDZ

Adventures in VeggieTown
Copyright © 2012 by Big Idea, Inc. VEGGIETALES.® character names, likenesses and other indicia are trademarks of Big Idea, Inc. All rights reserved.

Requests for information should be addressed to:
Zonderkidz, Grand Rapids, Michigan 49530

ISBN 978-0-310-72351-6

The Spoon in the Stone ISBN 9780310706267 (2005)
Field of Beans ISBN 9780310706281 (2005)
Frog Wars ISBN 9780310706274 (2005)

Written by: Doug Peterson
Illustrated by: Michael Moore
Original editor: Cindy Kenney
Editor: Mary Hassinger
Original art direction and design: Karen Poth
Cover design: Cindy Davis

Printed in China

12 13 14 15 16 /LPC/ 10 9 8 7 6 5 4 3 2

"Instead, whoever wants to become
great among you must be your servant."

(Mark 10:43)

The Spoon in the Stone

By Doug Peterson
Illustrated by Michael Moore

bigidea.com

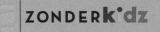

ZONDERVAN.com/
AUTHORTRACKER
follow your favorite authors

"Run, Junior, run!"

shouted Laura Carrot. "Leave the soccer ball behind!"

Junior Asparagus tore across Mr. Picklesheimer's backyard. Right behind him was a dog with ferocious fangs. The beast snarled and snapped.

Mr. Picklesheimer didn't like kids on his lawn so he bought a dog. Correction. He bought a creature that was part monster.

Junior ran for his life!

Just as the dog was about to attack, Junior leaped over the fence.
He was safe. But the soccer ball didn't make it. The dog tore it to pieces and gobbled it up.

Junior gulped. That soccer ball could have been him!

The Next Day...

Junior's mom told him that everyone was going to help Mr. Picklesheimer!
"What?" exclaimed Junior.

"Mr. Picklesheimer is getting old, and he needs help doing his yard work.
So our family and the Carrots are going to help him. God wants us to serve
others, Junior."

"Today?" Junior gasped. "Laura and I have more important things to do!"

"There's nothing more important than serving others," Mr. Asparagus said. "We need you home by one o'clock."

Junior sighed. He didn't like this—**AT ALL**.

Junior and Laura complained loudly in the Treasure Trove Bookstore in the heart of VeggieTown.

"Why should we help a grouchy old pickle?" Laura muttered. "We have more important things to do."

Mr. O'Malley couldn't help but overhear. "Aye, you're having the same problem a lad and lassie had in a storybook I once read. Let's see if I can find it," said the Irish potato who owned the store.

"It's somewhere in the *Serving Others* section, right next to the Scratch-and-Sniff Classics," he mumbled. "Ahhh, here it is. It's called *The Spoon in the Stone*."

Junior opened to the first page and saw a huge castle with a drawbridge. Standing in front of the castle were two Veggies in royal clothes.

Four words lifted up from the page into the air! They swirled around and around, growing larger and larger! Four simple words: **ONCE UPON A TIME**.

All At Once...

The four giant words swirled around Junior and Laura and...

WHOOOOOOOOOOOOOOOSHHHH!

Junior and Laura found themselves falling

down
   down
      down.

Everything was a blur as they zoomed straight through piles of large words...

and landed right in front of the castle door.

"Welcome to Hamalot!" shouted the tomato. "I'm Sir Irving, and this is my assistant, Sir Galaham. We run the Hamalot Hotel!"

"We like ham. **A LOT**," grinned the cucumber.

"We've been expecting you," said Sir Irving.

Junior and Laura blinked in surprise. "Huh?"

"Here's your apron," said Sir Galaham, "and your tray."

"Don't dilly-dally!" urged Sir Irving. "The hotel is packed with giants and ogres for this weekend's FE-FI-FO-FUN Trade Show. We have a shortage of servants!"

Irving and Galaham hurried them across a drawbridge. "There's much to do," Irving explained. "The Hamalot is the only place that leaves a ham on your pillow every evening instead of a mint."

Galaham grinned. "We like ham. **A LOT**."

"You can start on tables and deliver room service," explained Irving. He took Junior and Laura into the Hamalot Restaurant, which specialized in ham and beans, peanut butter and ham sandwiches, and banana-ham smoothies.

"You really do like ham. **A LOT**," observed Junior.

The restaurant was piled high with dirty dishes. Three lazy knights gobbled up food and played ping-pong with a hamball.

"That's Sir Nezzer, Sir Phillipe, and Sir Luntalot. They used to be hotel servants, but after they became knights, they decided they were too important to help around the hotel."

"These lazy knights used to be known as the Knights of the Round Table. But with no servants to clean up, the Round Table piled up with dirty dishes. So they switched tables and became the Knights of the Pool Table. Then they became the Knights of the Card Table. Now they're the Knights of the Ping-Pong Table," said Irving.

At That Very Second...

A pea ran up to Sir Irving and handed him a slip of paper.

"Here's your first job!" Irving said. "We've got a rush order of ham and bean soup. Deliver it to Room 53!"

The Knights of the Ping-Pong Table suddenly stopped playing. The hamball bounced off of the table and clunked Sir Nezzer in the helmet. It knocked his visor shut, on his tongue.

"Outh."

"Room 53?" gasped Sir Phillipe. "That's the dreaded giant Grizzle's room."

"Grizzle is in the Deluxe Dungeon Suite," noted Sir Luntalot. "And he's very dangerous."

"Thath right," said Sir Nezzer, whose tongue was still caught.

Junior and Laura looked at each other. "Maybe we'd better not bother him."

"Nonsense," said Sir Irving as he handed the tray of food to Junior. "You'll be fine! Besides, if you don't serve him this food, Grizzle will tear apart our hotel."

A Little While Later...

Laura knocked on the door to Room 53, and a giant pickle swung open the door. "WHAT TOOK YOU SO LONG?" he boomed.

If Junior had knees, they would've been shaking. A large dragon lurked behind the giant. Steam curled from its nose, which set off the smoke alarm.

The giant pickle roared and smashed the alarm into bits.

Junior cleared his throat and tried to be brave. "Your soup, sir."

The giant stared down at the bowl. "DA SPOON! WHERE'S DA SPOON?"

They forgot the spoon!

"I'll get it," Laura volunteered.

"*You* stay with *me*!" the giant roared. "If da little asparagus can't find da spoon before da Hamalot tower bell rings, den I'll have carrot stew instead."

Junior dashed back to the kitchen. All the spoons were caked solid with gunk!

"Please help me find a clean spoon!" Junior begged the Knights of the Ping-Pong Table.

"Sorry, we're knights, not servants," said Sir Luntalot.

"But God wants us to serve others!" Junior begged.

"Sorry," said Sir Nezzer. "We've got better things to do—like playing ping-pong."

Junior spotted a large spoon sticking out from a huge rock in the courtyard. He ran up to the spoon and grabbed the handle as the others gathered around him to see what would happen.

"That spoon is stuck in ancient oatmeal," explained Sir Galaham. "Many knights have tried to pull it out. But no one can do it."

Junior gave a mighty yank. The spoon wouldn't budge.

Then it happened. Junior gave a final tug, and the spoon slid from the stone, as smooth as butter. Trumpets sounded. Sunlight broke through the clouds. Everyone cheered!

Holding the spoon high like a sword, Junior dashed back into the hotel. But he was too late. The Hamalot tower bell was ringing.

After sprinting upstairs to Grizzle's room, Junior swung open the door. Was he too late to save his friend?

He held his breath...

"Oh hi, Junior!" chirped Laura. "Mr. Grizzle and I are having tea."

"Huh?"

"After I gave Mr. Grizzle some tea, he calmed down," Laura continued. "He's really quite friendly."

Junior held out the golden spoon. "Your spoon, Mr. Grizzle."

Grizzle's eyes widened. "It's da *famous* spoon in da stone!"

"They say whoever pulls the spoon from the stone has a true servant's heart," Galaham explained.

"God wants us to be a servant to others," Junior smiled.

Later, in the courtyard, Sir Galaham asked Junior and Laura to kneel before him.

"I dub thee Sir Junior and Lady Laura," he said, gently tapping them on the head with the spoon.

"Hold it!" shouted Sir Phillipe. "By making them a knight and a lady, they'll be too important to be our servants!"

"Don't worry," Junior told them.

"There's nothing more important than serving others," Laura added. "Even when you're a knight."

Sir Galaham grinned. "I like that. **A LOT**."

Just Then...

"Uh-oh," said Grizzle. "I think you're at **DA END** of da story."
"We'll miss you," Junior called.

In a Blink...

They were back in the Treasure Trove Bookstore.

"Well, how did you like the book?" asked Mr. O'Malley, shuffling over to them with sandwiches and pink lemonade. "Learn anything about serving others?"

Junior and Laura stared at the old Irish potato, still stunned by their adventure.

"Do **ALL** of your books do this?" Junior asked.

"Do what, laddie?" Mr. O'Malley asked as he set down the tray.

"You know. Pull you into the story?"

"Ahhh, all good stories pull you in," the potato said with a wink. "Here. Have a ham sandwich."

"Thanks," said Laura. "But we gotta get back home."

"Ahhh! That's right," agreed Mr. O'Malley. "You've got to help a neighbor, don't ya, lassie? But I thought you had more important things to do?"

Junior and Laura looked at each other.

"Nah," said Junior. "We can play later."

"Aye, that's the spirit!"

Mr. O'Malley watched as Junior and Laura dashed out the door. Then he sighed, took a big bite of ham sandwich, and smiled.

I sure like ham, he said to himself. **A LOT.**

In short, there's simply not
A more amazing spot
For happily serving other folks
Like a place called HAM-A-LOT!

Elijah went before the people and said,
"How long will you waver between two opinions?
If the LORD is God, follow him."

(1 Kings 18:21)

Field of Beans

By Doug Peterson
Illustrated by Michael Moore

bigidea.com

ZONDERVAN.com/
AUTHORTRACKER
follow your favorite authors

The bases were loaded in the last inning. Two outs.
Junior Asparagus stood at the plate with three balls and two strikes.
If Junior smacked a base hit, he would knock in the winning runs.
Lenny Carrot pitched the ball, everything seemed to move in slow motion.
The fans held their breath.
Junior swung.

"Steeeeerike three!" yelled the umpire. The mighty Junior struck out.

Back in the Dugout...

"Nice going, Asparagus. You lost us the game," grumbled Boog Pickle, the meanest kid on Junior's team. "If you carried a rabbit's foot for good luck, you wouldn't strike out."

"Everyone has something for good luck—except you," added Percy Pea.

It was true. Laura Carrot carried a lucky horseshoe. Boog Pickle tapped the bench three times with his bat every inning. And Jimmy and Jerry Gourd didn't wash their uniforms when the team was on a winning streak.

Judging by their smell, the team had been winning—a lot. Until today.

Junior didn't carry good luck charms because he didn't believe they had special powers. But now he wasn't so sure.

"Just because everyone else is doing something, doesn't make it right," said Reverend Archibald, the coach of Junior's team. "God wants us to follow him, not the crowd. He'll always lead us in the right direction."

Junior sighed.

"A lucky rabbit's foot can't change how a game turns out," Reverend Archibald added.

"I just don't know anymore," Junior muttered.

Later That Afternoon...

Junior wandered into the Treasure Trove Bookstore. "Mr. O'Malley, you're Irish," Junior said to the bookstore owner. "Do you have any lucky four-leaf clovers?"

"I'm afraid I don't, laddie," grinned the potato. "But I do have a storybook you might like to read."

Mr. O'Malley dug through a shelf, yanking out books left and right. "The book is somewhere in the Sticking-Up-for-What-You-Believe-In section, right next to the Pop-up Math Books."

"Ahhh, here's the one. It's called *Field of Beans*." When Junior opened the first page, he saw a huge stadium packed with thousands of baseball fans.

At That Very Moment...

Four giant words floated up from the stands of the stadium. Four simple words: ONCE UPON A TIME.

Suddenly...

The four words swirled around Junior. They whirled and twirled and **WHOOOOOOOOOOSH!**

Junior tumbled over

and over

and over.

He somersaulted through the stands…and landed right in the stadium.
"You're just in time, Coach!" said a funny-looking grape, running up to Junior.
Junior was baffled. "Why did you call me Coach?"
"Because you're my coach, Coach!" said the grape. "My name is Eli, and this is
the biggest game of the year!"

The stadium was packed with screaming, chanting fans.

"Everyone is rooting for the other team, but that's okay," said Eli. "I don't mind going against the crowd when they're rooting for the Relics."

"Who are the Relics?" Junior asked.

"You don't know who the Baal City Relics are?" Eli exclaimed. "The Relics have won the championship for the last forty years."

Eli explained that everyone wanted to play for the Relics because they had such a great record.

"Why do the Relics keep winning so much?" asked Junior.

"Well, if you ask them, they will tell you it's because of the idols they worship," Eli explained.

"They worship idols?" Junior asked. "What kind of idols?"

"Lucky idols," said Eli. "You see that bean over there? His name is Shoehorn Joe. He's a legend. He wears that little gold-plated shoehorn in every game because he thinks it will make him win."

"Why don't YOU start wearing a lucky charm like the Relics?" Junior asked.

"I don't believe in 'em," Eli said. "I follow the Lord, the only one, true God. I don't trust in lucky charms, I trust in God. And today's the big showdown between the Relics and the Lord."

The crowd roared, as hundreds of beans ran out on the field. They jumped up and down and tackled each other. They really knocked themselves out.

"Is that THE TEAM?" Junior asked. He was a little worried about the odds.

"Yep, those are the players for Baal City. All 450 of them. You sure don't know much about this game, do ya kid. Tell you what. Try listening to the announcers. They'll tell you what's happening in the game."

He motioned toward a nearby booth where a tomato and a cucumber were hunched behind their microphones.

"Welcome to the match-up of the century!" said one announcer. "My name is Bob the Tomato."

"…and I'm Larry the Cucumber. It's a beautiful day for a Baal game. Not a cloud in the sky!"

"Uh, Larry…It hasn't rained for three years," noted Bob. "A cloud in the sky would be nice."

"Oh, right. Drat," said Larry. "But have we got a game for you! It's the Mount Carmel Dodgers versus the Baal City Relics. Let's get ready to rumble!"

"Tell us a little about today's game, Larry," said Bob.

"Sure thing, Bobbo. Both teams are going to wheel out a HUGE barbeque grill and pile it high with their favorite ballpark snacks. The Relics are going to rely on their lucky idols to get their charcoal started. And Eli is going to ask the Lord to start his grill. Whoever gets their grill lit first–wins! Not to mention they get a whole bunch of delicious hot dogs and nachos with melty, bubbly, warm cheese on top."

The game kicked off with Baal City. The Relics rolled their grill out into the middle of the field. Then players bowed before the grill and began rubbing their lucky charms and praying to their idols.

"Answer us!" they shouted.

No answer.

"Come on, idol, light our fire!" they yelled.

No fire.

"Please! Just a spark!"

No spark.

One Half Hour Later...

"It looks like the Baal City Relics are in big trouble, Larry," Bob reported. "They're calling up players from their bullpen."

Larry wasn't paying attention. He was too busy standing up and singing.

"Take me out to the Baal Game. Take me out to the crowd.
Buy me some peanuts and matzo dough. Follow God! It's the best way to go.
So it's root, root, root for our Lord's team! If you do, you'll be glad that you came!
Cuz it's one! Two! Three strikes you're out! At the old Baal Game!"

Larry was right. The Baal City Relics were striking out. They still couldn't get a fire to light in their grill.

No matter how hard the Relics rubbed their lucky charms and prayed to their idols, their grill wouldn't start. Shoehorn Joe rubbed the gold plating right off his shoehorn, but still the fire wouldn't start.

It was finally the Dodgers' turn.

"What can you tell us about the Dodgers, Larry?" asked Bob.

"Well, Bobbo, they only have one player on their team, but he's an all-star," said Larry. "His name is Eli, and he's good at dodging trouble from the League Commissioner. With a lifetime average of 356, he leads the league in the wilderness."

"No wonder he was named most valuable player two years in a row!" noted Bob.

"That's right, Bobbo," said Larry. "He was in the minors for two seasons, but he worked his way up to being a Major Prophet in record time."

"He's being coached by a little asparagus," Bob said. "But what's this?" Bob said. "I can't believe it, Larry!"

Eli soaked the grill with kiwi, watermelon, and grape juice three separate times. Coach Junior had a fit.

"What are you doing?" Junior yelled. "The charcoal's not going to burn if you dump juice on it! Use lighter fluid!"

"The Lord can start this grill on fire, even when it's soaked with juice," Eli explained. "He can do anything!"

Junior just shook his head.

Then Eli stepped forward and boldly began to pray.

"Lord, you are the God of Abraham, Isaac, and Israel. Let everyone know that you are God in Baal City. Answer me, Lord. Then these people will know that you are the one and only God."

The crowd went so quiet that you could hear a mosquito sneeze.

"Achoo!"

"God bless you," whispered Larry.

And then it happened...

A brilliant bolt of lightning blasted the grill, sending the hot dogs and pretzels toward the hungry fans.

The crowd roared.

"That grill is outta here!" shouted Bob.

"And the fans are going crazy!" yelled Larry. "With God's help, Eli stood up against the crowd and pulled off an amazing victory! That's one for the Book!"

After a Long Celebration...

Two words suddenly appeared on the scoreboard. Two simple words:

THE END.

Junior knew what that meant. The story was over.

"You were incredible," Junior said to Eli.

"Not me, Junior, the Lord. Just remember to follow God and not the crowd. He will do incredible things in your life, too."

All at Once...

Junior felt himself being pulled toward the scoreboard. Closer and closer and...

The next thing he knew, Junior found himself back in the Treasure Trove Bookstore. The roaring crowd was still ringing in his ears.

The Next Day...

Junior stepped up to bat. Once again, Boog Pickle blocked his way.

"I hope you got a lucky charm," snarled Boog.

"Sorry, Boog," Junior said. "Lucky charms don't have any power."

"If good luck charms don't have power, then how did Laura Carrot just get a big hit?"

Laura hurried from first base over to second. But then she slowed down.

"Hey! What's wrong with her?" Boog muttered.

"Yer out!" yelled the umpire as Laura looked back to see the horseshoes fall from her pocket.

"These goofy things slowed me down," she complained. "They weigh a ton! I'm not carrying them around any more. Lucky charms don't really work, anyway."

From That Day On...

Boog didn't bother Junior again.

Sometimes Junior got hits. Sometimes he didn't. Sometimes his team won. Sometimes they didn't. But Junior always followed God both on and off the field. As for Mr. O'Malley, he was always in the stands, singing this song:

Take me out to the Baal Game. Take me out to the crowd.

Buy me some peanuts and matzo dough. Follow God! It's the best way to go.

So it's root, root, root for our Lord's team! If you do, you'll be glad that you came!

Cuz it's one! Two! Three strikes you're out! At the old Baal Game!

"Be strong and take heart, all you who hope in the LORD."

(Psalm 31:24)

Frog Wars

By Cindy Kenney and Doug Peterson
Illustrated by Michael Moore

bigidea.com

ZONDERVAN.com/
AUTHORTRACKER
follow your favorite authors

Junior Asparagus had been trying to learn how to play the tuba all day. But the noise coming out of it sounded like a sick water buffalo with a pail on its head. **BWOOOOOOOOMBABLUUUURRRTT–BLATT!!!** echoed through the house.

Fifteen Minutes Later...

Junior slammed his tuba on the floor.

"I quit!" he shouted as his mom rushed into the room.

"Junior, you love music. And this is the fourth instrument you've tried this month," she said.

"Ya, but I'm no good at it," he puffed.

"Perhaps it's because you're using The **Advanced** Guide to Playing Tubas on your first day. Even if God made you musically gifted, it takes perseverance before you can play well."

"Percy-fear-ants? God never gave them to me."

"Perseverance means 'keep trying; don't give up hope.'"

"Hope?" he muttered. "Nope. Don't got it."

Later That Afternoon...

Junior wandered into the Treasure Trove Bookstore.

"Do you have any books on how to play the violin?" he asked Mr. O'Malley, the Irish potato who owned the store.

Mr. O'Malley peered at Junior. "I thought you were learning to play the tuba, laddie."

"Apparently, tubas and I weren't made for each other."

Mr. O'Malley's eyes lit up. "I have the perfect book for you."

O'Malley climbed a tall ladder to find the book. "It's somewhere in the *Never-Say-Die* section, next to the Self-Help Comic Books." Finally, he found it: *Frog Wars*.

Junior opened the book and saw a beautiful palace in the middle of a desert. Workers lifted giant statues that looked like huge stone frogs.

At That Very Moment...

Four giant words floated up from the first page of the book. Four simple words: ONCE UPON A TIME.

The four giant words swirled around Junior, and...
WHOOOOOOOOOOOOOOOOOOOSH!
Junior slid **down**
                    down
                              down.
But as he slid down the giant page, the words moved up!
They said: **A long time ago, in a land far, far away . . .**

EPISODE IV:
A REALLY, REALLY NEW HOPE
Dark Visor and his evil empire are
forcing the people of Salon to be
his slaves. He's making them build temples
to the great frog god, Ribbit. But the one
true God is rising up a hero to rescue them...

After sliding down the words, Junior crash-landed inside the *Frog Wars* book! "Where did you come from?" asked a cucumber slave, hopping up to Junior. "He fell from outer space," said a blueberry. "Hello, Space Boy. I'm Princess Hair-Spraya, and this is Cuke Sandwalker."

Junior stared at the cucumber's wig. Then he looked at Princess Hair-Spraya with a baffled look on his face. "You have cinnamon buns on your ears."

"Where else do you suggest I carry them?" she frowned. "I don't have hands, you know."

"Don't worry, we won't hurt you. We were captured from Salon, which is on the other side of the Big Frog Pond. We were brought here to be Dark Visor's slaves," the cucumber explained.

Just then, two other slaves peeked out from behind a frog statue. "Is it safe to come out, Master Cuke?" asked a pea dressed in gold.

"C'mon out," Cuke Sandwalker called.

The two peas cautiously approached the little asparagus. "I'm Sweet-Pea-3-Oh," said one of the peas. "This is Achoo Bless-U. We're slaves, too."

"Are you the one who's come to free our people?" asked Princess Hair-Spraya.

"I don't think so," said Junior, a little confused.

"We've been asking the one, true God to send someone who will lead us out of here. You must be the one!" said Cuke Sandwalker. "Follow us, Space Boy."

Junior stayed close behind as Cuke and his friends rushed through the palace and into the throne room.

The king, a zucchini named Dark Visor, sat on a great frog throne. His visor made his breathing sound funny.

"He hates the sunlight," whispered Achoo Bless-U.

"What's with all the frogs?" Junior asked.

"Dark Visor believes in a frog god called Ribbit," Princess Hair-Spraya told him. "He doesn't believe the true God will send someone to help us."

"So go ahead and tell him," nudged Cuke.

"Tell him what?" asked Junior.

"Tell him to let God's people go free!"

Trembling With Fear...

Junior moved toward the king.

"What do you want?" Dark Visor bellowed after lifting his visor.

"Let the people of Salon go free," Junior squeaked.

"NO!" thundered the king so loudly it caused his visor to slam shut.

"Okay, I gave it a shot," Junior shrugged and turned to leave.

"Wait!" said Cuke Sandwalker. "You hardly tried at all!"

"Trying isn't really my thing," Junior added as he ran for the door.

At That Very Moment...

. . . a guy named Mo stormed into the room carrying a walking stick. The big round tomato was on a mission.

"Stick with me," Mo told Junior. "We won't give up until Dark Visor gives in." Mo turned to the king and spoke. "My name is Mo! And God wants you to let his people go!"

But Dark Visor only snarled at him with a heavy breath.

"**Whmmmimmtwyouttodsiiiiiiii**."

"Huh?" everyone gasped.

"Lift your visor, and try it again," suggested Sweet-Pea-3-Oh.

The king flung his head back to open the visor and roared, "When I'm through with you, you will all turn to the dark side!"

Dark Visor would not let the slaves go free. But did Mo give up?

Nope! He had hope and would not give up, because he put his faith in the Lord.

Mo warned Dark Visor that God would not be pleased, but the big zucchini didn't care. So Mo threatened to turn all the water in the kingdom to juice, and soon purple liquid bubbled from every drinking fountain in the city.

"This guy's really good," Cuke Sandwalker whispered to Junior.

Day After Day After Day...

Mo threatened the king with God's anger, but the king refused to let the people go. Junior just wanted to quit and go home.

But Mo encouraged him to stay. "God wants us to have faith in him. That means doing our best and *not* giving up," he told Junior. Then Mo shouted, "My name is Mo! And God wants you to let his people go!"

"No way, Jose," Dark Visor replied as he sipped his juice.

So the tomato warned the king that God would send plagues on the land. And plagues were scary things like...

…days and days of doing the Hokey Pokey.

…swarms of dust bunnies.

…a drought of pizza and ice cream.

…and the invasion of FROGS!

Even though the king worshiped the frog Ribbit, unwanted, *real* frogs turned up everywhere! The king found them in his cereal bowl. In his pajamas. Even on his throne! But Dark Visor would not let God's people go free.

Many Days Later...

"Isn't it time to give up?" asked Cuke Sandwalker.

"What do you think, Junior?" Mo asked.

Junior thought about it. *God wants us to put our hope in him and keep trying!*

"Anything else we can try?" Junior asked.

Mo smiled, and they prayed to God for help.

Then God sent a deep darkness to fall upon the land.

"Is this what you meant when you talked about turning to the dark side?"
Achoo Bless-U teased the king.

Finally...

...an amazing thing happened. Dark Visor heard that familiar voice... "My name is Mo! And God wants you to let his people go!"

"I can't see anything in the dark!" he groaned as he flipped his visor up just as he was about to sit on a frog. "Ribbit has turned against me in my time of need.

"Alright! Let the slaves go free, and take these frogs with you!" the king shouted.

The clouds began to part as the slaves marched out of the land. Junior rode in a wagon with his new friends, except there was no room for Cuke Sandwalker.

"Use the horse, Cuke!" said the princess.

"Good thinking," smiled the cucumber.

But Before the Slaves Could Get Away...

Dark Visor slammed down the lid of his visor and sent his army to chase after the slaves.

"**IchkabildGoafrtthslvsfslnan!**"

"Huh?"

He flipped his visor back open and shouted, "I changed my mind! Go after the slaves from Salon!"

The Empire struck back!

The slaves were trapped in front of the Big Frog Pond with no way to get across. In front of the slaves was the treacherous pond muck. The king's army was quickly approaching them. The people from Salon were afraid.

Junior was scared, too. But did he give up? Nope! He had hope! He saw how God continued to watch over the people again and again. He knew they had to trust God in a mighty way.

"Don't give up!" Junior shouted.

Then Mo called out: "You will see how the Lord will save you!"

Suddenly...

The lily pads in the pond came together and turned to stone while the waters parted to each side. God created a pathway so the slaves could get to the other side.

But Dark Visor's army was right behind them.

Did Junior and Mo give up?

Nope! They had hope!

As the Sun Began To Rise...

    The slaves arrived on the other side of the pond, and the lily pads returned to normal. The pond filled with water and muck. The soldiers sank into tons of mud and water, and clamored to shore.

    "It's not easy being mean," said the king, pulling himself out of the muck.

    "Ribbit," said a frog behind him.

    With the army defeated, the slaves cheered on the opposite shore.

And Then It Happened...

Two words suddenly popped out of the sand...along with several frogs.
Two simple words: **THE END**.

"Thanks for not giving up, Junior!" said Mo.

"Thanks for teaching me to never give up!" replied Junior.

"Goodbye, Space Boy!" called Princess Hair-Spraya.

"Be strong and never lose hope," added Cuke Sandwalker. "May the Lord be
with you."

The two giant words swirled around Junior like a desert whirlwind. The next
thing Junior knew, he was back in the Treasure Trove Bookstore, shaking sand from
his hat.

In the Store...

Mr. O'Malley shuffled out of the back room when he heard the bell above the door jingle.

Junior told Mr. O'Malley all about his adventure. Dark Visor. The frogs. Mo.

"Aye, but what did you learn?" asked Mr. O'Malley.

"That God wants us to have hope in him. And that we shouldn't give up, even when things get difficult," he said. "By the way, do you have *The **Beginner's** Guide to Playing Tubas?*"

"I sure do, laddie!" Mr. O'Malley chuckled. "Let it be my gift to you."

"Thanks!" Junior beamed as he hopped out of the store.

Then, Mr. O'Malley said to himself, *New hope you have. Happy that makes me.*

Want to read a real story about having hope in the Lord?
Read the story of Moses in Exodus, chapters 1 to 15, in the Bible.